# A missing prize is no laughing matter.

Molly took the tissue from her pocket. She studied the funny answers to her riddles.

"I really want to win and get on TV," she whispered to Cam's father.

"What about the silver plate?" he asked. "Don't you want to win that?"

Cam looked at the small table at the edge of the stage. The green cloth was still on the table. There was nothing on top of the green cloth.

"What plate?" Cam asked. "The silver plate is gone."

"Someone must have stolen it," Eric said.

"How could anyone do that?" Mr. Jansen asked. "We're all facing the stage and that table. How could someone take the plate without being seen?"

"I think Eric is right," Cam said. "I think it was stolen and we have to find out what happened right now. The longer we wait, the easier it will be for the thief to get away."

# CAM JANSEN

CASE #34

## and the
## Joke House
## Mystery

**David A. Adler**
Illustrated by Joy Allen

PUFFIN BOOKS

PUFFIN BOOKS
An imprint of Penguin Random House LLC
375 Hudson Street
New York, New York 10014

First published in the United States of America by Viking,
an imprint of Penguin Young Readers Group, 2014
Published by Puffin Books, an imprint of Penguin Random House LLC, 2015

THE LIBRARY OF CONGRESS HAS CATALOGED THE VIKING EDITION AS FOLLOWS:
Adler, David A.
Cam Jansen and the Joke House mystery / by David A. Adler ; illustrated by Joy Allen.
p. cm.
Summary: While Cam's Aunt Molly is competing in a comedy contest, the expensive plate the
winner will receive disappears and Cam and Eric set out to find it before the contest is over.
ISBN 978-670-01262-6 (hardcover)
[1. Mystery and detective stories. 2. Stealing—Fiction. 3. Jokes—Fiction. 4. Contests—Fiction.]
I. Allen, Joy, illustrator. II. Title.
PZ7.A2615Caag 2014 [Fic]—dc23 2013046783

Puffin Books ISBN 978-0-14-751235-2

Printed in the United States of America

3 5 7 9 10 8 6 4

For my grandson Andrew

—D.A.A.


To Curt, my funny guy!

—J.A.

# CAM JANSEN

## and the
## Joke House
## Mystery

# Chapter One

"I'm in big trouble," Cam Jansen's aunt Molly said. "I remember the riddle questions, but I don't remember the funny answers."

Cam, her father, Aunt Molly, and Cam's best friend Eric Shelton were at the Joke House. Aunt Molly was there to compete in a joke-telling contest. Cam, Eric, and Mr. Jansen had come along to cheer for her.

"I really want to win," Aunt Molly said, "but I don't even remember why the chicken crossed the road."

"Don't worry," Mr. Jansen told her. "When you get onstage you'll remember everything."

"The winner gets the chance to tell jokes

on television. If I win, I'll be famous," Aunt Molly said.

Cam's father pointed to a small table at the edge of the stage. There was a green cloth on the table that reached the floor. On top of the table was a large silver plate.

Cam's father told Molly, "You'll also win that plate. It's worth a lot of money."

A tall man was standing by Cam's table. "Hi, I'm Kevin," he said. "I'll be your server tonight."

Kevin gave everyone a menu. "I'll be back to take your orders soon."

Kevin went to the next table.

Cam, Eric, and Mr. Jansen looked at their menus.

Aunt Molly tried to remember why the chicken crossed the road.

"I think the chicken was on its way to school. That's why it crossed the road. Or maybe the chicken was going shopping. Whenever I go shopping, no matter where I am, I always have to cross the road. All the good stores are always across the strect."

"It's not the story of the chicken's whole life. It's just a joke," Eric told Aunt Molly. "The chicken crossed the road to get to the other side."

"Oh," Aunt Molly said. "To get to the other side. I have to remember that."

Cam closed her eyes. She said, *"Click!"*

"Here are some more chicken jokes," Cam said, with her eyes still closed. "The chicken crossed the playground to get to the other slide. It crossed the amusement park to get to the other ride. And the orange stopped in the middle of the road because it ran out of juice."

"Hey! Those are the jokes I'm going to tell. How do you know them?" Aunt Molly asked.

Cam opened her eyes and said, "I looked at your joke book. I have pictures in my head of every page of that book."

Cam has a photographic memory. It's as if she has a camera in her head and pictures of everything she's seen. Cam blinks her eyes and says, *"Click!"* when she wants to look at one of the pictures. Cam says, *"Click!"* is the sound her mental camera makes.

"Do you know this one?" Eric asked. "What do you call a chicken that crosses the road, rolls in some dirt, and then crosses back again?"

"That's easy," Cam said, and laughed. "That chicken is a dirty double-crosser."

Cam's real name is Jennifer. When she was young, some people called her "Red," because she has red hair. Then they found out about her amazing memory and started calling her "The Camera." Soon "The Camera" became just Cam.

"What would you like?" Kevin asked. He was standing by the table again.

"I'll have a large glass of iced tea," Aunt Molly said.

"I'll have a cup of hot tea," Mr. Jansen told Kevin.

"I want a glass of orange juice and some cookies, please," Cam said.

"Me, too," Eric told Kevin. "Juice and cookies, please."

A man with a long mustache curled at each end walked to the center of the stage. He stood by the microphone.

"Welcome to the Joke House. I'm Gary Gold," the man said. "Tonight one comedian will win a chance for fame and fortune. The winner will be invited to perform on my show, *The Gary Gold Comedy Hour*. The winner will also get a silver plate with the engraved message 'Winner, Comedy Night at the Joke House.' Your laughter and applause

will determine who wins. We'll begin in just a few minutes."

"Fame and fortune," Aunt Molly said. "That's what I want. I just have to remember my jokes."

Molly took a tissue and pen from her purse. "Other side," she wrote on the tissue, "other slide, other ride, ran out of juice," and "dirty double-crosser."

Kevin took two glasses of juice off his tray and gave them to Cam and Eric. He gave them each a large plate of cookies. He gave Mr. Jansen and Aunt Molly their teas. Then he asked, "Do you know why you don't tell an egg chicken riddles?"

The lights dimmed. The show was about to begin.

"You don't tell an egg chicken riddles because it might crack up," Kevin said. "And do you know how to fit six elephants in a car? You have two sit in the front, three in the back, and one in the cup holder."

Aunt Molly said, "But an elephant is too big to fit in a cup holder."

"That's the joke," Cam explained.

"You can use that joke if you want," Kevin told Molly. "I'm also a comedian. But Gary won't let me enter the contest because I work here."

"Thank you," Molly said. "I will."

"When elephants go on a car trip," Molly wrote on her tissue, "the car has to have a cup holder."

"Good evening," Gary Gold said into the microphone. "It's time to start the contest. It's time to laugh!"

# Chapter Two

"I can't eat all these cookies," Eric said to Mr. Jansen and Aunt Molly. "You should have some."

Mr. Jansen took a cookie. Molly took two.

"Now, let's meet the people who will make you laugh," Gary Gold said into the microphone. "First, we have Uncle Sid."

A man with long, curly brown hair and a yellow baseball cap stood. He held up a large cloth bag.

"What's in the bag?" Cam asked.

"He's a prop comedian," her father answered.

"What's that?"

"You'll see."

"Next meet Granny Janie."

A woman wearing a white wig and a large
pair of eyeglasses stood. She waved a cane.

Eric whispered, "That's not her real hair.
She's not really old. She's pretending."

"Now meet Molly Jansen."

Aunt Molly stood and waved. She had a cookie in each hand.

"She's waving oatmeal raisin cookies!" somcone shouted.

Aunt Molly looked at her hands. She saw the cookies and laughed. She took a big bite out of one of the cookies and sat down.

"She's funny," someone at the next table said.

Gary Gold called the names of three more comedians. They each stood. Then he called for Uncle Sid to come onto the stage.

People applauded.

Uncle Sid carried his big cloth bag onto the stage. He opened the bag and looked into it. Then he looked at all the people sitting in the Joke House.

"Do you want to know what's in my bag?" Uncle Sid shouted.

He held his hand to his ear.

"What's in the bag?" people shouted back.

"I'm glad you asked," Uncle Sid said.

He took a strange cardboard clock from his bag. The twelve numbers were bunched together at the bottom, and the clock had no hands.

"This is a clock for people who don't care what time it is."

Mr. Jansen and a few others laughed.

Uncle Sid dropped the clock on the floor of the stage and took out a coffee cup. He showed everyone the large hole in the bottom of the cup.

"This is for people who don't like coffee."

Cam, Eric, Mr. Jansen, and a lot of other people laughed. Even Aunt Molly laughed.

Uncle Sid took a large comb from his bag. The teeth of the comb were missing.

"This comb is for bald people."

The laughter got louder.

Eric whispered, "Why would a bald person need a comb?"

"That's the joke," Mr. Jansen told him.

Molly took the tissue from her pocket. She studied the funny answers to her riddles.

"I really want to win and get on TV," she whispered to Cam's father.

"What about the silver plate?" he asked. "Don't you want to win that?"

Cam looked at the small table at the edge of the stage. The green cloth was still on the table. There was nothing on top of the green cloth.

"What plate?" Cam asked. "The silver plate is gone."

# Chapter Three

"Someone must have stolen it," Eric said.

"How could anyone do that?" Mr. Jansen asked. "We're all facing the stage and that table. How could someone take the plate without being seen?"

"I think Mr. Gold moved it," Aunt Molly said. "He brought it into the kitchen. Maybe someone in there is polishing the plate so it will look shiny when he gives it to the winner."

"I think Eric is right," Cam said. "I think it was stolen and we have to find out what happened right now. The longer we wait, the easier it will be for the thief to get away."

Cam got up.

"I'm going to ask Mr. Gold what happened to the plate."

Eric got up, too. They walked along the side of the room, past several tables, until they were in front, right by the edge of the stage.

Gary Gold was standing at the back of the stage, just in front of the curtain. Cam waved to him. When Gary Gold didn't respond Cam waved wildly with both hands.

Gary Gold looked at Cam. Then he looked away.

"He's pretending not to see you," Eric whispered.

Uncle Sid took a large book from his bag. He opened it. Its pages were blank.

"This book is for people who don't like to read."

Cam whispered, "I'll wait until Uncle Sid is done. Then I'll tell Mr. Gold about the plate."

Uncle Sid took a large fake chicken from his bag. He pulled on it to show everyone that it was made of rubber. He dropped the chicken on the floor of the stage, and it bounced.

"Take a look at the eggs this chicken laid."

Uncle Sid took two rubber balls from his bag and bounced them. He threw the first ball to Gary Gold, who caught it.

Gary Gold bowed, and lots of people cheered.

Sid threw the second ball high over Gary Gold's head. The ball hit the curtain and fell to the floor. Gary Gold bent down to get the ball.

*Rip!*

People laughed and pointed at Gary Gold's pants.

"His pants didn't really tear," Eric whispered to Cam. "It was Uncle Sid."

Sid held a piece of cloth by the microphone. He tore it some more.

*RIP!*

The laughter got louder.

Uncle Sid dropped the cloth on the floor. He reached into his bag again. He lifted the bag and looked in.

"It's empty," he said. "I guess I'm done."

People applauded.

Uncle Sid bowed and started to walk off the stage.

Gary Gold walked to the microphone. He looked at the props Uncle Sid had dropped on the floor.

"Wait," he told Sid. "You can't go until you've cleaned up your mess."

Eric said, "That's what my mother always tells me."

Uncle Sid picked up all his props and put them into his cloth bag. He bowed again and left the stage.

Gary Gold said, "Maybe Uncle Sid will win the chance to take his rubber chicken on television. Maybe he'll take home this large silver plate."

Gary Gold said that without turning to look. He pointed to the empty table on the side of the stage.

Uncle Sid put the cloth bag under his table and sat down.

Gary Gold said, "Or maybe our next comedian will win the prize. Please welcome a funny woman who is so old, she's old enough to be her own mother. Please welcome Granny Janie."

Granny Janie got up slowly. She had a small wool shawl draped over her shoulders. She shook and stumbled and leaned on her cane as she walked toward the stage.

"Wait," Cam called out. "Something is missing."

"Sit down, please," Gary Gold told Cam.

"You pointed to the table with the silver plate. The plate is gone."

"I should know where it is," Gary Gold said. "I put it there myself."

Gary Gold turned and looked at the table on the side of the stage.

"It's gone!" Gary Gold said, and hurried to the small table. He lifted the green cloth and looked under it. He moved the curtain aside. Behind it was a bare stone wall.

"The silver plate is gone," he said. "Some-one stole it."

Granny Janie stood by the microphone.

"There have been three big changes in me as I got older," she said. "My hair turned white, and I keep forgetting things."

"That's just two," someone called out. "What's the third big change?"

Janie scratched her head and said, "I forgot."

Gary Gold walked off the stage. "I've got to find that missing plate," he mumbled as he went past Cam's table.

# Chapter Four

Gary Gold hurried through the big room, past all the people sitting at tables. Cam and Eric followed him.

"Helen," he said to the woman standing by the entrance. "Has anyone left here carrying a large silver plate?"

"People keep coming in. They all want to be here for the contest. No one has left."

"Thank you. I'll check the back door."

Gary Gold turned and saw Cam and Eric. "What are you doing?"

Cam said, "I'm the one who told you the plate was missing."

"She's Cam Jansen," Eric told Mr. Gold. "She has an amazing photographic memory. She solves mysteries."

"I don't need a child detective," Gary Gold mumbled as he hurried back through the big room. "I need that plate."

"My old friend doesn't hear so well," Granny Janie told the people in the Joke House. "We were going out and I said she should take a coat. I told her it was windy. 'No,' she said. 'It's Thursday.'"

No one laughed.

"It's a joke," Janie explained. "I said 'windy' and she thought I said 'Wednesday.'"

Gary Gold walked quietly along the side of the room. He passed the small empty table at the side of the stage. He pushed through two large swinging doors and went into the kitchen.

Cam and Eric quietly followed him.

In the center of the kitchen was a long blue table. On it were a few plates of cakes and cookies.

"Hi, Boss," a short, plump man said. He was wearing a large white chef's cap and a white jacket.

Behind the man, there was a stove, a refrigerator, and a door with a window. Along one side of the kitchen were coats hanging on hooks, and several cubbies. Along the other side was another man washing dishes in two big metal sinks. Large metal counters were attached to the side of the sinks.

"I see trees through that window," Cam whispered. "That door goes outside."

"Hi, Hal," Gary Gold said to the man wear-

ing the chef's cap. "Did anyone walk past you and go out the back door?"

Hal shook his head.

"What about you, Stan," Gary Gold asked the dishwasher. "Did you see anyone leave?"

Stan shook his head.

"I've been standing here since six o'clock," he said, "and no one went through that door."

"We came at eight," Eric whispered, "and when we got here that plate was still on the small table."

A server walked in carrying a large tray of dirty dishes. She took the dishes off her tray

and put them on one of the counters by the sinks.

"Susan, what do you need?" Hal asked.

Susan took a small pad from her back pocket and read from it.

"One order of spaghetti and meatballs, a chicken salad, a cup of vegetable soup, and two teas."

She put her tray on the blue table. She poured two cups of hot water and put them on her tray. Beside each cup she placed a tea bag. Hal prepared the food and put the plates on her tray.

Gary Gold took a cell phone from his jacket pocket, pressed a few buttons, and waited.

"There's been a robbery at the Joke House," he said into his phone. "A valuable silver plate was taken."

Hal gasped.

Gary Gold listened for a moment. Then he said, "Please come in through the side door."

Gary Gold put his cell phone away.

"Susan, when the police get here, try to keep them from upsetting our guests."

"Sure, Boss."

"Now I've got to get going. I've got to introduce the next act."

He turned and saw Cam and Eric.

"Why are you still here?"

"We'll solve this mystery," Eric told him. "We'll find that silver plate."

"The police will find it. Please just find your seats. You don't want to miss the next act. It's a funny woman named Molly Jansen."

# Chapter Five

"The thief is one of the people in the Joke House," Cam whispered. "Somehow no one saw him take the plate, and no one saw him hide it."

"Him or her," Eric told Cam. "The thief might be a woman."

Cam and Eric returned to their table.

"Did you find the plate?" Cam's father asked.

"Not yet," Eric answered. "But we will."

Gary Gold was standing on the stage.

"It's time for our next comedian," he said into the microphone. "Please welcome a funny woman named Molly Jansen."

People applauded. Cam looked across the table at Aunt Molly. She was clapping, too.

"Molly," Mr. Jansen told her. "You're clapping for yourself."

"Oh! Is it my turn?"

Molly walked onto the stage. She stood by the microphone and smiled.

"Tell some jokes," Mr. Jansen called out.

"Oh, jokes."

Molly thought for a moment and then asked, "Why is the chicken a dirty double-crosser? It's because it ran out of juice."

No onc laughed.

"No, that's not right," Molly said. "It's because it might crack up."

"What is she talking about?" a woman at the next table asked.

"She's pretending to be mixed up," the man next to her answered, "and it's funny."

Cam whispered to Eric, "Aunt Molly isn't pretending."

"Wait! Wait!" Molly said. "I wrote the jokes down."

She took the tissue from her pocket and looked at it.

"This doesn't have the riddle questions on it. It just has the answers."

She turned the tissue over.

"More answers. But that's okay. The answers are the funny part."

She looked at her tissue and read from it.

"To get to the other ride."

She looked up and said, "That's why the chicken crossed something. I just don't know what it crossed."

People laughed.

"Did you know that elephants like to go on car trips?" Molly asked. "But the car has to have a cup holder."

More people laughed.

"Listen to this," Molly said. "An orange crossed the road and then it stopped. Do you know why it stopped?"

Molly waited.

No one told her why the orange stopped in the middle of the road, so Molly looked at her tissue.

"It stopped to get to the other side," she read. "Oh, no, to get to the other slide or ride, or something.

"Oh, and did I tell you about the dirty double-crossing chicken?"

"You told us," someone called out.

Molly turned and looked at Gary Gold.

"That's all I have on my tissue," she told him, "so I think I'm done."

Gary Gold stood next to Aunt Molly.

"Let's hear it for Molly Jansen."

Lots of people applauded. Mr. Jansen, Cam, and Eric clapped the loudest. Molly bowed, waved her tissue, and walked off the stage.

"Look at that," Eric whispered. "Aunt Molly walked right past the small table. Everyone who walks on or off the stage walks past it."

Cam closed her eyes. She said, *"Click!"*

"Uncle Sid walked past the table, and he had that large bag of props," Cam said with her eyes still closed.

Aunt Molly returned to her seat.

"You were great," Mr. Jansen told her.

"I should have practiced more," Molly said. "Then I wouldn't have mixed up all the jokes."

Cam opened her eyes. She turned and looked at the bag next to Uncle Sid.

"Maybe Uncle Sid took it," Cam whispered to Eric. "We have to sneak over there and look in his bag. We'll do it when the next comedian is telling jokes. Maybe then we won't get caught."

Eric said, "Maybe then we'll find the silver plate."

# Chapter Six

"I hope you're ready for some knock, knock fun," Gary Gold said. "Please welcome Knock, Knock Norm."

A young man in an orange jacket that was much too big for him walked onto the stage.

He tapped twice onto the microphone.

*Knock, knock!*

"Who's there?" people in the audience called out.

"It's me, Knock, Knock Norm."

He tapped again on the microphone.

*Knock, knock!*

"Who's there?"

"Hatch."

"Hatch who?" people in the audience asked.

"Please, cover your nose when you sneeze."

Some people laughed.

Eric said, "I don't get it."

Mr. Jansen explained, "'Hatch who' sounds like *achoo*, the noise you make when you sneeze."

*Knock, knock!*

Mr. Jansen, Molly, and lots of other people called out, "Who's there?"

"This is our chance," Cam whispered.

Norm said, "Lettuce."

Cam quietly left her seat. Eric followed her. They crawled to where Uncle Sid was sitting.

"Lettuce who?"

"Lettuce in. It's cold out here."

Cam and Eric crawled under the table.

"It's dark here," Eric whispered.

"Sh!" Cam told him.

Cam reached into the bag and took out
the book with blank pages. She took out the
rubber chicken, coffee cup, cardboard clock,
comb, and two rubber balls.

"There's no plate," Cam whispered.

"No plate?" Eric asked.

He crawled over to look in the bag. On
the way, he touched someone's shoe.

"Hey! Who's under there?"

Suddenly several people bent down and looked under the table.

"What are you doing with my bag?" Uncle Sid asked.

Cam and Eric sat up and banged their heads on the bottom of the table.

"Get out of there!" Uncle Sid said.

Cam and Eric crawled out. Cam told everyone at the table about the missing prize.

"You thought I took it?" Uncle Sid asked. "I wouldn't steal that plate. I want to win it."

Cam said, "It's just that you walked past the small table at the edge of the stage and your bag is big enough to hide the plate."

Uncle Sid said, "Lots of people walked past that stage."

"Look!" someone at one of the other tables said. "The police are here."

Two police officers walked through the kitchen door. One was a man with a brown mustache. The other was a woman with curly black hair. They walked past the small table at the edge of the stage.

"Knock, knock," Norm said quickly.

"Who's there?" lots of people asked.

"Donna," Norm answered. "Donna arrest me for telling bad jokes."

Gary Gold stepped onto the stage. He stood by the microphone and said, "Let's hear it for Knock, Knock Norm."

A few people applauded. The others at the Joke House were watching the police officers.

Norm went to his seat.

"There will be a short break in our show," Gary Gold said.

Cam looked at the police officers. She looked at Gary Gold. Then she looked at the small table at the edge of the stage.

Cam closed her eyes and said, *"Click!"*

She said, *"Click!"* again.

"Eric," Cam said, and opened her eyes. "I think I know where to find the missing plate."

# Chapter Seven

Gary Gold and the police officers were on their way to the entrance to the Joke House.

"You told us the plate was here when the show started," one of the officers said to Gary Gold as they walked past Cam's table. "There are lots of people here. Anyone could have taken it."

"Not anyone," Cam told Eric. "Only people who walked past that small table could have taken it."

"I saw you and Eric walk past it on your way to the kitchen," Mr. Jansen said.

"But we didn't take it," Eric told him.

"I know that."

"Mr. Gold and the police officers walked past it," Eric said. "I know they didn't take it."

Eric thought for a moment. Then he said, "Uncle Sid, Granny Janie, Aunt Molly, and Knock, Knock Norm also walked past the table. Maybe Granny Janie has it. Maybe she hid it in her shawl."

"No," Cam said. "By the time Janie went onstage, the plate was already gone."

"I went after Janie," Aunt Molly said. "So I couldn't have taken it."

Just then Susan went through the door to the kitchen. She was carrying a large tray filled with dirty cups and plates.

Cam said, "The servers walk past that small table every time they go into the kitchen."

"Kevin serves us," Eric said. "Susan serves the tables next to ours."

Eric looked around the room.

"There are two other servers."

"It would be easy for one of them to take the plate," Cam said. "When a server walks past the small table, he could just grab the plate and put it on his tray."

Eric said, "Susan and one of the other servers are women. So maybe *she* grabbed the plate and put it on *her* tray."

"Maybe," Cam said. "And then the thief would have to hide the plate."

Cam closed her eyes. She said, *"Click!"*

Cam quickly opened her eyes.

"There are cubbies in the kitchen. I bet each server has one. And each cubby is big enough to hide the plate."

Eric got up.

"Let's go look," he said.

Cam got up, too.

"You can't look in people's cubbies," Mr. Jansen told Cam and Eric. "Whatever is in them is private."

"We could go to the police," Cam said. "We can tell them where to find the plate."

"I'm going with you," Mr. Jansen said.

Cam, Eric, and Mr. Jansen started toward the side of the big room.

"Hey!" Aunt Molly called. "Wait for me! I'm coming, too."

They all went to the entrance to the Joke
House. The police officers and Gary Gold
were there. They were talking to Helen. Cam
told them where she thought the silver plate
was hidden.

Gary Gold said, "I'll tell all the servers to meet me in the kitchen. If one of them took the plate, we'll find it."

They all walked toward the kitchen. As they went through the big room, Gary Gold told each of the servers to come with him.

Gary Gold, the two police officers, Mr. Jansen, Molly, Hal, Stan, Susan, Kevin, and

the two other servers all crowded into the kitchen.

Gary Gold introduced the two police officers.

"This is Officer Jacob Berger," he said. "His partner is Officer Beth Cooper."

Gary Gold told them all about the missing prize and where Cam thought it was hidden.

Everyone was quiet for a moment. Then one of the servers looked down, like he was embarrassed.

"It was me," Kevin said. "I'll show you where I hid the plate and I'll tell you why I took it."

# Chapter Eight

Kevin walked by the stove and refrigerator and past a few hanging coats. He reached into one of the cubbies and took out a sweater. He unfolded the sweater and there was the silver plate. He gave it to Gary Gold.

"I'm not a thief," Kevin said. "I'm a comedian. I'm really very funny. I wanted to have a chance just like anyone else to win this plate and be on television. I know I would have won."

"No one who works here can enter the contest," Gary Gold said. "That's the rule."

"You stole something," Officer Berger told Kevin, "so you are a thief."

Officer Cooper unhooked a set of hand-cuffs from her belt.

"You'll have to come with us."

"Please," Gary Gold said to the police. "I have my plate. Don't arrest him."

Officer Cooper put the handcuffs away.

"Thank you," Kevin said.

"But you can't work here anymore," Gary Gold told Kevin. "Take your things and leave.

You've also lost your chance to ever tell jokes at the Joke House."

Kevin emptied his cubby. He took his jacket off the hook. He opened the back door and left.

"Thank you for getting this plate back," Gary Gold said to the police officers.

"We didn't find your plate and we didn't catch the thief," Officer Berger said. "It was this red-haired girl. She solved this mystery."

"Thanks for your help," Officer Cooper said to Cam.

Eric said, "Cam has a photographic memory. She used it to solve this mystery."

"A photo what?" Officer Cooper asked.

"Show them," Eric said.

Cam looked at everyone standing in the kitchen. She said, "*Click!*" and closed her eyes.

"Turn around," Cam's father told her. "That way no one will think you're peeking."

Cam turned around.

"Officer Berger," Cam said, "your badge number is 2164. There is some mud on the

toe of your right shoe. And Mr. Gold, the
bottom button of your vest was sewn on with
different-colored thread than the others. It
must have been replaced."

Gary Gold looked down at his vest.

"Oh, my, you're right!" he said.

He gave Officer Berger a paper napkin to
wipe the mud off his shoe.

"Officer Cooper," Cam said. "The red nail polish on two of the middle fingers of your left hand is chipped."

"Is it?" her partner asked.

Officer Cooper looked at the fingernails of her left hand.

"Yes."

"Wow!" Gary Gold said to Cam. "Could you and your friend come on my television show and demonstrate your amazing memory?"

Cam and Eric looked at Mr. Jansen.

"You may go, Cam. Eric, I'm sure your parents will also let you go."

"Cam and Eric are too young to go by themselves, so I'll bring them," Aunt Molly told Gary Gold. "Since I'll be there, maybe I can go on your show, too, and tell some jokes."

"That would be nice," Gary Gold said.

Officers Berger and Cooper thanked Cam again and left the Joke House. Hal and Stan went back to their work in the kitchen. The others returned to the big room.

Gary Gold stood by the microphone again. He introduced the last two comedians. Cam and Eric listened, ate their cookies, drank their juice, and laughed.

When the comedians were done, Gary Gold brought all six onstage. One by one, he asked the people in the Joke House to clap for their favorite.

Lots of people clapped for Aunt Molly. But more people clapped for Uncle Sid.

He won the silver plate and the chance to appear on television.

"That's okay," Aunt Molly said. "Thanks to Cam, I'll be on television anyway. And this time, I'll practice so I won't be all mixed up."

"No, don't do that," Mr. Jansen told his sister. "Mixed up is funny. You're funny."

Cam said, "You're my very funny aunt even without practicing."

"And you're my very best friend," Eric told Cam, "my very amazing best friend."

# A Cam Jansen Memory Game

Take another look at the picture oppo-
site page 1. Study it. Blink your eyes
and say, *"Click!"* Then turn back here and
answer the questions at the bottom of the
page. Please, first study the picture, *then*
look at the questions.

1. What is printed on the stage curtain?

2. How many people are sitting at the
   table with Aunt Molly?

3. Are the two plates of cookies, glasses of
   juice, and cups of tea on the table?

4. Can you see the large silver WINNER
   plate?

5. Is Cam smiling?